OUT OF THE FIRES

A Journal of Resilience and Recovery After Disaster

by Carrie Lara, PsyD
illustrated by Colleen Larmour

Magination Press • Washington, DC
American Psychological Association

For the children and families of Sonoma County, where we remain resilient and stand together community strong—*Carrie Lara*

For the people and nature affected by wildfires and for those who work to protect and repair our earth from the devastating effects of climate change —*Colleen Larmour*

Books for Kids From the
American Psychological Association

Text copyright © 2023 by Carrie Lara. Illustrations copyright © 2023 by Colleen Larmour. Published in 2023 by Magination Press, an imprint of the American Psychological Association. All rights reserved. Except as permitted under the United States Copyright Act of 1976, no part of this publication may be reproduced or distributed in any form or by any means, or stored in a database or retrieval system, without the prior written permission of the publisher.

Magination Press is a registered trademark of the American Psychological Association. Order books at maginationpress.org, or call 1-800-374-2721.

Book design by Rachel Ross and Gwen Grafft
Printed by Worzalla, Stevens Point, WI

Cataloguing-in-Publication Data is available at the Library of Congress.
ISBN: 9781433840692
eISBN: 9781433840708
LCCN (print): 2022023889
LCCN (ebook): 2022023890

Manufactured in the United States of America
10 9 8 7 6 5 4 3 2 1

October 8, 2017 was a day like no other for Sonoma County, California. My family and I woke to a neighbor pounding on our door at 2 am. The sky was orange and smoke filled the air. In the far distance we could see the brighter glow of fire as the wind blew fiercely. The whole block was packing up and evacuating. We headed to my uncle and aunt's house for a few days, closer to the ocean. There the sky was clear and the air safe to breathe. We were lucky; when we returned, our house was unharmed. But we know many people who were not so lucky. In just a few days, the Tubbs Fire of Sonoma County had burned down a total of 5,643 structures, the majority of them homes. Many people lost everything and had to rebuild, start over. It was a traumatic and tragic experience for the whole community.

It felt as though the community was at a standstill yet busy at the same time while the fight went on. The hospitals and community centers had pop-up support groups. Firefighters and first responders from around the country, even international teams, fought the fires. My husband as a county worker was assigned to one of the evacuation sites where he helped families with supplies and resources. Twenty-two days after it started the fire was contained, and life had to resume despite the miles of destruction, and many people still trying to find stability. It was hard, but also good to go back to our "normal" routines. We all wore N95 masks to protect ourselves from the toxins in the air as we went about our days. It was a surreal scene.

There were many stories of strength and resilience even in the tragedy. The school where my mother was principal held a parade led by firefighters and police officers on the first day back. A local celebrity chef had teams feeding the heroes on the front line. Groups of people teamed up with animal shelters to go into the burned areas to find lost pets, provide care, and reunite them with families. But it was still hard. Friends and family members reported feelings of anxiety whenever there were high winds or a storm. As a therapist I was working with children and families who were dealing with loss due to the wildfire. I felt really lucky to be able to provide this support, but also lucky that I still had a home. Working so closely with the community I saw the multiple layers of trauma and loss associated with natural disasters. During a disaster, community wherever it may be found can be a symbol of resilience.

Natural disasters are occurring more frequently with each year, whether they are wildfires, floods, or storms. With changes in climate contributing to significant drought, rising sea levels, melting ice caps, and other changes, we are seeing more severe and unpredictable weather events across the world. During the same month in 2017, we were also surrounded in my area by the Nuns Fire in Napa and Sonoma counties, the Atlas Fire in Napa and Solano counties and the Redwood Valley Fire of Mendocino County. Many more have occurred since that first year throughout California and in other areas around the world. We now call the fall months "fire season." In 2019 we went through it again in Sonoma County with the Glass and Lighting fires. This time the fire came within a mile (two blocks and a chicken farm) from our house, but again we were lucky to be able to return home. Once more, the community banded together. We even had hashtags to show our resilience (#sonomacountystrong, #windsorstrong).

But we can be strong individually too. The definition of resilience is the ability to adapt when faced with a problem or challenge. We make mistakes as human beings, and we learn from them. We can even learn from unexpected events, like loss or disaster. We practice adaptability by talking about our feelings, accepting that reactions and responses to problems are normal, and trying to problem solve. The more we practice these skills, the more we build our adaptability. That is the key to resilience. You may be feeling lots of different emotions, like the main character of this story. There is no right or wrong way to feel. Allow yourself to acknowledge those feelings and reactions, and then try to find a way to use your strengths to work through it. It is my hope that with this book, you can follow one kid's journey as he not only experiences a natural disaster but is able to work through his responses and reactions and find his resiliency. In the back of the book there are tools and resources for building resilience and strengths.

—Carrie Lara

PART 1:

RETURN TO SCHOOL

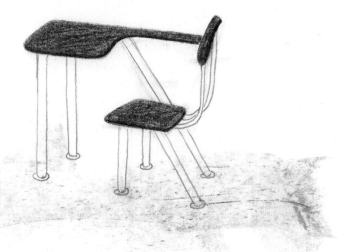

SCHOOL

We returned to school today.

It felt weird since we haven't been to class for a couple of weeks. The teachers made signs to welcome us back.

WELCOME BACK

TO SCHOOL

We are glad you are here

We missed you

The principal, Ms. Higgins, held an assembly first thing in the morning. I sat with Noel, Avery, and Jorge in the bleachers. It felt good to be with my friends again.

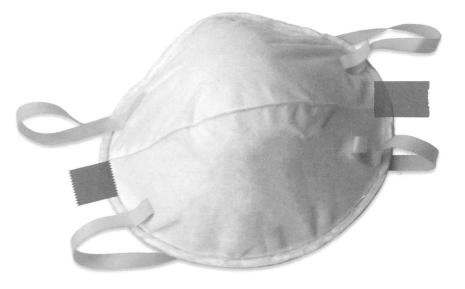

The kids all around me kept giggling and pointing at the teachers wearing their N95 masks, whispering how funny we all look. I don't feel like giggling. The mask is uncomfortable, and it's a good thing it hides my face.

They can't see that I am **not** smiling.

Ms. Higgins talked to us about resilience:

"Resilience means to be strong, to know that things can happen that are hard or scary, but we are all safe and okay. We are stronger because of the hard things that can happen sometimes."

The teachers passed out a paper while we listened.

She tells us she is going to break us into groups to meet with the school counselor throughout the day, so we can talk more about what happened. She says "talking can help." My stomach drops. I am not sure I want to talk about it.

Ms. Higgins keeps talking, but now I hear only bits and pieces.

I am thinking about how I can escape.

I hear her say my name for group D. "Group D will be right after lunch." Suddenly, I'm not hungry at all.

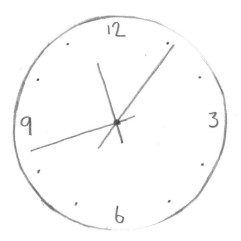

In class I keep looking at the clock, counting the minutes until lunch...

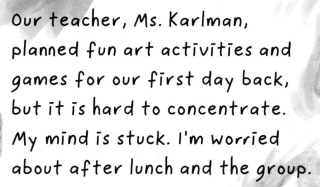

Our teacher, Ms. Karlman,
planned fun art activities and
games for our first day back,
but it is hard to concentrate.
My mind is stuck. I'm worried
about after lunch and the group.

I start having fun after a while,
especially with the art. I love to draw—
it is a good distraction.

I even smile a couple times. Noel made a joke about an interrupting cow and I laughed out loud!

Then it was lunchtime. Mom packed my favorite, a peanut butter and blackberry jam sandwich. I eat slowly. I don't want to do the group next!

Maybe if I eat slow enough, lunch won't ever end?

The bell rings and I have to go to the library for my group's turn to meet with Ms. Ortiz, the counselor.

She seems nice and told us that we can talk about whatever we want. "This is a safe place. All feelings, thoughts, and questions are welcome."

I sit quietly.

Ms. Ortiz handed us a piece of paper with faces on it. Each face had a different feeling under it.

"Whatever we are feeling is okay," she said. "You can circle the face that maybe you are feeling right now."

How do you feel right now?

Sad   Tired   Happy   Numb   Angry   Anxious

Other kids in group began to talk about what happened for them and their families the last couple of weeks while we weren't in school. Sometimes they pointed to one of the feeling faces while they shared.

When it is my turn, I shake my head, my stomach feels sick — my lips stick together. Ms. Ortiz says...

Ms. Ortiz says that sometimes things can be too hard to talk about, and there are other ways to get out what we may be feeling, like:

> drawing,
> writing,
> listening to music,
> or doing worksheets.

"Some people even like to do physical things like taking walks or exercising."

Ms. Ortiz hands us a piece of paper with questions on it. "This is a worksheet that can help you figure out what works for you. Maybe fill it out at home and see what you come up with." I look at the paper and read the first line.

When I feel worried, my body feels like

_____

_____.

"Let's all stand up for a minute," said Ms. Ortiz.

"Reach up to the ceiling and spread your fingers wide."

"Now take a deep breath...hold it—
1 – 2 – 3 – 4 – 5 – now let it out slowly..."

I feel some of my muscles start to relax as the air leaves my lungs. We do that three more times and the group is over.

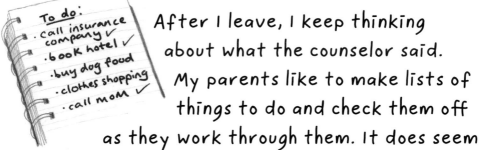

To do:
- call insurance company ✓
- book hotel ✓
- buy dog food
- clothes shopping
- call mom ✓

After I leave, I keep thinking about what the counselor said. My parents like to make lists of things to do and check them off as they work through them. It does seem to help them feel better, especially the last couple of weeks.

My little sister Kayleen talks, and talks...and TALKS! To anybody who will listen. She likes to listen to music too.

So what could I do?

I look at Ms. Ortiz's worksheet again.

When I feel worried, it helps me to

_____

_____.

I thought about what I like to do. I like to write in my journal. And I like to draw. Maybe, I can write in here about it. Maybe if I try, it will help me too.

PART 2:

WHEN THE FIRES CAME

Let me tell you about that one day everything was there, and then there was nothing. It was gone.

Everything was gone.

MATH
LITERATURE
HISTORY
SCIENCE

It was a normal Sunday. Kayleen and I played soccer in the backyard and worked on our homework. My parents did laundry and we went to bed. Everything seemed normal. I never thought it would be any different....

B+

We found
ourselves in a
large gymnasium.

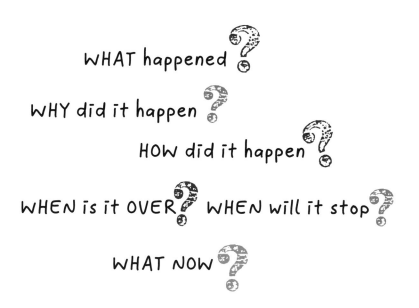

Surrounded by all those people,
we felt all alone.

Pictures kept flashing in my head. The
house, the smoke in the sky, the orange
glow above the trees, the line of cars
leaving the neighborhood...I felt so
confused. So many questions...

WHAT happened ?

WHY did it happen ?

HOW did it happen ?

WHEN is it OVER ?   WHEN will it stop ?

WHAT NOW ?

Nice people with name tag badges brought us food and water, and some blankets to snuggle with on the cots. I remember holding my little sister while we waited.

She kept petting our dog, Layla. It felt good to be holding them both, and to know they were with me. Layla's fur was warm and soft.

News came in bits and pieces, through phones, radios, or other people coming in. The firefighters kept going, but the fire remained too strong, the winds too high. A street was reported gone, a school, a whole neighborhood. It felt like forever.

...erage.

In some countries
history, what news media and the public
has considered "newsworthy" has met different definitions. For example, mid-twen-

More recently, th
mains on political a
ever, the news medi

found in
ch being
etroleum,
ıvier than
y sinks be-

ı semi-sol-
ater, as in
da, where
bitumen.
ı a sticky,
/hich is so
heated or

ınts of oil
ςh the hy-
more fluid
ılled extra

called un-
em from
ditional
Canada
ated 3.6
·a-heavy
world's

ient-rich
f Mexico
the large
ıg to the
which it

organic
ςequent
ı mud.
ιecame
essure

·ature
ı win-
rature
rogen,
ıre the
ıgh the

ıts such
e large
g to the
·hich it

Wildfires Rage Across Counties, Leaving Nothing Behind in Their Path as Thousands Flee for Safety

Thousands of people were forced to evacuate in the middle of the night as fire ripped through the area. Many people woke up to the smell of smoke and an orange glow on the horizon, some only having minutes to get themselves and their families in the car before the fire was upon their properties. Stories are pouring in of people driving through the fire to escape the neighborhood, and a few jumping in their swimming pools to be safe.

The combination of high drought and strong winds led to a perfect storm. The wildfires continued to grow with the 60 mph winds encouraging them, pushing them across the freeway and expanding into the city. Whole neighborhoods were swallowed by the morning. First responders are continuing to fight the fires through the day, while emergency personnel check on residents at the evacuation sites all over town.

Area co_____ in m_____ disappe_

We met some other families while we waited. One family shared how they had lived in the same house for three generations, ever since their ancestors moved to the area from Italy.

Another man and woman shared that they had just bought their first home.

We shared our family stories too. We told them about the day we got Layla, and how excited we were. We love playing with her in the backyard and teaching her new tricks. Everyone hoped for the best, played games, and waited it out together. We felt like an instant community.

Finally, it was over. But it wasn't. It was all gone: our home, our street, our whole neighborhood. My favorite baseball mitt,

the quilt my grandma made me,

the family photo albums.

One day it was all there, and then it was all gone.

A Hazy Horizon, Smoke and Ash Everywhere, Create Eerie Scene

People in the affected area and neighboring counties woke up to devastation caused by the wildfires. Ash covered the ground, an orange-gray hue blanketed the horizon, and smoke clouded the air. County officials have issued an air quality advisory, urging everyone to limit exposure as much as possible, and wear an N95 mask if attempting to go outside.

"The air feels thick," stated a local community member while standing outside a coffee shop waiting for news that he would be able to get back to his neighborhood, the orange-gray hue in the sky behind him.

Mom and Dad went to look at our street while we stayed with Grandma and Grandpa. After they came back, I heard them talking to Grandpa when they thought I couldn't hear, but I hear everything.

My emotions exploded:

sadness, anger, despair, pain, loss.
Hopelessness.

What do we do now?

I watched my parents
as they struggled
to figure out our
next steps. I could
tell they felt just
as worried and
stressed as I did.

Kayleen kept asking about the neighborhood cats. "Do you think they're all right?" she asked.

"Animals are smart. They probably figured out an escape," I tried to comfort her. I didn't want our parents to worry about us too. "And there are people out looking for them, to give them food and take them to the shelter so their families can find them."

PART 3:

A COUPLE WEEKS LATER

Time seems to go both *fast* and s l o w.

We have been staying at a hotel, but Mom and Dad found us a house to rent. We move in on Saturday.

It also helps that school is open again. It helps to see my friends and my teacher, and have stuff to do.

Resiliency in the Midst of Destruction

Area residents have rallied around each other showing determination and resilience in the wake of the wildfires that began ravaging the county just a few days ago.

At evacuation centers, volunteers and county workers are providing ongoing supplies, support, and connection to temporary lodging. As evacuations are being lifted, people are able to return to their neighborhoods to see what is left. Some non-profit groups are working to locate and care for lost pets while families are located and reunified with their furry friends.

There is a sense of community and camaraderie throughout the county.

It's almost like normal, except everyone is wearing masks for protection from the smoke and ash in the air, and nobody can stop talking about the fires.

I wish people would stop talking about it. I don't want to think about it anymore. I want it to be normal.

Writing and drawing in my journal has helped a bit. I don't feel like talking about it yet, but I brought my journal to share my story with Ms. Ortiz, and she liked it.

She talks to me about feelings and how to

"COPE."

I do have lots of feelings!

Sometimes I feel angry.
Angry it is all gone. Angry at the fire.
Angry at nature. Angry at people.
Angry at the world.

I yell sometimes at my friends,
teachers, and parents, but I
don't mean to.

Sometimes I just feel angry...
It's easiest to be angry.

Sometimes I feel sad.

Sad that my house is gone, sad that my friend's family had to move away, sad to see my parents upset and stressed, sad the trees are gone, the flowers, the grass.

It's hardest to be sad.

Sometimes I
feel scared.

I hear a siren in
the distance...is it
happening again?

I smell smoke...where
is it coming from?

Sometimes I dream of an
orange glow and hot air, and
I wake up, my heart racing.

Sometimes I feel lost.

Lost from home, lost from my neighborhood, lost in my day.

I move from moment to moment—surviving.

People talk about their future. What is my future?

When are we going home?

Sometimes I feel angry, sad, scared, and lost, all at the same moment. Sometimes I just feel numb.

And sometimes...I don't know how to feel.

But sometimes I feel happy again.

How do you feel right now?

Sad   Tired   Happy   Numb   Angry   Anxious

I feel happy to see Noel, Avery, Jorge, and even the teachers at school.

I feel happy, comforted,
and loved as my family and I
watch a movie on pizza night.

I feel happy and proud to see the signs around town thanking the firefighters and first responders.

I feel happy playing with Layla and Kayleen at the park, the skies clear and the sun shining.

I feel happy and grateful for each day, each person, and everything I do have, even on the days that I feel angry.

It's okay to be happy too.

PART 4:

A YEAR LATER

Lots of time has passed now, a whole year.

Homes Starting to Pop Up in Neighborhoods Devastated by the Wildfires Last Year

Construction companies have moved in, and wood frames have been erected around the neighborhoods previously flattened by the wildfires last year.

Many families have had to move on, and for every building going up a "For Sale" sign is seen on another lot nearby. However, community members describe a sense of anticipation, excitement, and rejuvenation as the buildings are finally starting to be rebuilt. "I drive through here every morning on my way to work," a local community member reported, pointing to the street behind her. "Seeing the building structures start to go up finally, it is just really great to see."

New houses are popping up everywhere.

We get to move home again soon!

I miss our old house, but Mom let me keep her old key for my journal.

The community is rebuilding. It feels good to see everything regrowing too—new trees, new grass, and wildflowers everywhere!

This flower is actually called a fireweed, and the name comes from its ability to quickly colonize areas burned by fire!

Wildflowers Blanket the Countryside, Showing a Rebirth After the Wildfires

A dazzling display of color has taken over the hillsides and meadows of what was recently ashes. It is being noted by nature lovers as the most significant growth for wildflowers in the area in many decades. Local scientists describe the process of the fire removing the grass, plants, and many years of built-up debris from dead trees and foliage that strips the soil of the nutrients. The fire not only provides a natural clearing of that area, but the ash also provides nutrients to the soil.

However it came about, the community has welcomed the beauty with open arms, embracing nature's resiliency in strengthening their own.

People still talk about the fires. But it's not as hard now and talking about it is good. It helps me move through all those sticky emotions and build strength. Strength in myself, in each other, in our community.

In school we learned about fire prevention and how important it is to take extra care with fire safety during a drought and all times of the year.

How to Help Keep
Your Home Safe

1 Clear any bushes or shrubs close to the building structure. Create a safety zone.

2 Help your parents with raking leaves, and putting them in the yard waste bin.

3 Help conserve water: take shorter showers, turn off the sink when not using it, use reusable water to water the garden.

4 Remind your parents to clear out the gutters regularly.

5 Be prepared—have a family evacuation plan and "go bag."

Sometimes other things happen around the world that remind me about the wildfires, and I can feel all the feelings again. But I use my strength to help move through it. I use my writing and drawing to help me, or I talk to my parents about it.

Like when I saw in the news about the flood in the midwest that put whole towns underwater.

Or when I overheard my parents talking about the tsunami in the Pacific and the earthquake in Asia.

People had to leave their homes just like we did. They lost everything and had to rebuild too. It's scary to hear about stuff happening in other places, but I also know how strong we can all be.

Our class put together messages of strength and hope recently to send to students like us in Australia because there were huge fires that burned everything.

I sent the worksheet paper the counselor had given us.

Helping others is a good way to help ourselves feel better too.

Wildfires Cover Much of the Continent of Australia, Making it Difficult to Find Refuge for Human and Animal Alike

Video and pictures of koalas and kangaroos attempting to find refuge are pouring in, as the residents attempt to help. "It's difficult to get out to where the animals are," said one local animal expert, "given the spread and dangers of the fire. But we are doing what we can." The fires continue to rage around the country having a devastating impact.

While the majority of the country of Australia is on fire, many people continue to debate the effect of climate change. Scientists discuss the role of climate change in natural catastrophic events. "Drought and higher temperatures make it easier for fires to start and spread," said one environmental scientist. "As the fires burn through large areas of forest and fields, it creates more climate-changing carbon that is pushed into the atmosphere."

I've learned things can happen in our lives that we can't know will happen. Sometimes there isn't even a reason why either, which makes it seem so much harder. And we can't know how we will respond. One day everything was there, and the next it was gone.

It can be very hard, but it is okay to feel all the feelings together.

It's okay to be angry or sad, lost or scared. I don't feel so mixed up anymore. I still feel scared sometimes when I hear the sirens, but I also feel pride when I see the firetruck drive by, the brave firefighters going to protect us.

It is important that we don't judge ourselves or others for our different feelings and responses. Sometimes we live day by day, moment to moment.

Let me tell you about that one day everything was there, and then there was nothing.

RESIL

But I am still here, and I am strong.
I am

RESILIENCY & COPING WORKSHEET

Resiliency is the ability to bounce back, survive, recover, and grow stronger through the challenges we face in life. Let's work together and practice your resiliency skills! Please answer the following questions:

EMOTIONS
Mixed emotions are a normal response to experiencing a trauma, loss, or challenging stressor. Often, we can feel sadness, anger, anxiety, or even nothing.

When I feel anxious or nervous I _____

Someone I can talk to when I am nervous is _____

Something I can do is _____

When I am angry I _____

Something I can do instead is _____

When I am sad I _____

What can I do when I am sad is _____

PROBLEM SOLVING

When I face a problem, do I focus on the problem or look for solutions? _____

What helps me to refocus? _____

Is there a person that helps me to refocus? _____

What is a problem I had before and how did I overcome it? _____

What did I learn from that problem? _____

SELF CARE & GRATITUDE

What are 5 things I can do to take care of myself?

_____
_____
_____

IDEAS: Take a walk   Take a bath

Read   Listen to music   Play an instrument

Draw   Try something new

Take a break   Practice mindfulness

What is something I do well? _____

What are 5 things I am grateful for? _____

_____

HELPING OTHERS

Helping others is a really good way of building resilience. What are some ways that I can help others using my strengths and from what I've learned?

_____
_____
_____
_____
_____
_____
_____
_____

ADDITIONAL RESOURCES

Below is a list of books, articles, and other online resources that may provide additional information for you and your parents.

Fires, Fire Safety, and Disaster Preparedness
Books

Popovici, D. (2021). *The fox and the forest fire*. Chronicle Kids.
In this picture book, when a forest fire approaches, a boy and his mom have to flee their home in the woods. Eventually animals, including his fox friend, return to the forest, and the boy and his mom begin to rebuild. For ages 5–8.

Thiessen, M. (2016). *Extreme wildfire: Smoke jumpers, high-tech gear, survival tactics, and the extraordinary science of fire*. National Geographic Kids.
Nonfiction book all about wildfires, their impact on the environment, and their prevention and containment. For ages 8–12.

Online Resources

ASPCA Disaster Preparedness
aspca.org/pet-care/general-pet-care/disaster-preparedness
Steps to be prepared to keep your pets safe before an emergency or natural disaster.

Ready.gov Build a Kit Game
ready.gov/kids/family-emergency-planning/build-a-kit
In this game, progress through different levels as you pick items to build an emergency kit.

Ready.gov Disaster Master Game: Wildfire
ready.gov/kids/games/data/dm-english/wildfire.html
In this game, help campers in Colorado stay safe during a wildfire.

ScienceTrek: Wildfires!
sciencetrek.org/sciencetrek/topics/wildfire
An informative collection of videos from Idaho Public Television, exploring wildfire basics, types of wildfires, what happens after a fire, and more. For ages 8–10.

Trauma and Resilience
Books

Holmes, M. M. (2000). *A terrible thing happened: A story for children who have witnessed violence or trauma*. Magination Press.
A gently told and tenderly illustrated story for children who have witnessed any kind of violent or traumatic episode, including natural disasters such as floods or fire. An afterword by Sasha J. Mudlaff written for parents and other caregivers offers extensive suggestions for helping traumatized children, including a list of other sources that focus on specific events. For ages 4–8.

Moss, W. L. (2016). *Bounce back: How to be a resilient kid*. Magination Press.
Filled with quizzes, advice, and practical strategies to help you build resiliency skills. For ages 8–12.

Neimark, J. (2016). *The hugging tree: A story about resilience.* **Magination Press.**
Tells the story of a little tree growing alone on a cliff, by a vast and mighty sea. Through thundering storms and the cold of winter, the tree holds fast. For ages 4–8.

Straus, S. F. (2013). *Healing days: A guide for children who have experienced trauma.* **Magination Press.**
A useful book to read with a parent, caregiver, or therapist, *Healing Days* is a sensitive and reassuring story intended for children who have experienced trauma and covers the feelings, thoughts, and behaviors that many kids have after a bad and scary thing happens. Kids will begin to understand their response to the trauma and learn some strategies for feeling safer, more relaxed, and more confident. For ages 6–11.

The Climate Crisis and Coping with Eco-Anxiety

After reading this book, you may have questions about climate change. Here are some additional resources with more information, ideas for taking action, and ways to cope with big feelings.

Books

Celano, M. & Collins, M. (2023). *Something happened to our planet: Kids tackle the climate crisis.* **Magination Press.**
Written to help parents to begin conversations with their children about a challenging and important topic, *Something Happened to Our Planet* describes the narrator's efforts to help the planet, with her friends, by advocating for re-usable plates at her school. Includes extensive endmatter with a glossary, sample dialogues, and guidance for discussing climate change with children. For ages 4–8.

Davenport, L. (2021). *All the feelings under the sun: How to deal with climate change.* **Magination Press.**
Informative text and activities to give readers the tools they need to manage their anxiety about the climate crisis and work toward making change. For ages 11–14.

Drimmer, S. (2019). *Ultimate weatherpedia.* **National Geographic Kids.**
A reference book about all kinds of weather phenomena filled with fun facts, photos, and graphics. Includes features on drought, heat waves, and the effect of climate change on weather. For ages 7–10.

Toner, J. B. (2021). *What to do when the news scares you: A kid's guide to understanding current events.* **Magination Press.**
A workbook to help with children's feelings of anxiety around current events and what is portrayed in the news. For ages 6–12.

Online Resources

Above the Noise: Does Climate Change Cause Extreme Weather?
pbslearningmedia.org/resource/climate-weather-kqed/does-climate-change-cause-extreme-weather-above-the-noise/
This video explores how scientists are investigating the role climate change plays in extreme weather events. For ages 11–18.

Climate Change on National Geographic Kids
kids.nationalgeographic.com/science/article/climate-change
All about climate change, including a glossary and ideas for what you can do to make a difference. For ages 6–13.

NASA Climate Time Machine
https://climatekids.nasa.gov/time-machine/
Interactive visualizations allow you to see how the climate is changing over time—including Arctic sea ice, the sea level, carbon dioxide, and the global temperature. For ages 9–12.

For Parents, Caregivers, and Teachers

Books

Wilson, R. & Lyons, L. (2013). *Anxious kids, anxious parents: 7 ways to stop the worry cycle and raise courageous and independent children*. HCI Books.

Wilson, R. & Lyons, L. (2013). *Playing with anxiety: Casey's guide for teens and kids*. HCI Books.

Online Resources

Alvord, M. K., Gurwitch, R., Martin, J., & Palomares, R.S. (created 2012, January 24. Last updated 2020, August 26). Resilience guide for parents and teachers. APA. **apa.org/topics/resilience-guide-parents**

Pedersen, S. (2017, January 24). Raising resilient kids. ICAN. **icanaz.org/raising-resilient-kids/**

PTSD in children: Know the signs, symptoms, and how to get help (2018, February 23). Georgetown Behavioral Health Institute. **georgetownbehavioral.com/blog/ptsd-in-children-how-to-get-help**

Tartakovsky, M. (2016, May 17). 10 tips for raising resilient kids. PsychCentral. **psychcentral.com/lib/10-tips-for-raising-resilient-kids#1**

Tips for managing your distress related to wildfires. (Created 2011, August 1. Last reviewed 2021, September 16). APA. **apa.org/topics/disasters-response/wildfires-tips**

Climate-aware Therapists
The Climate Psychiatry Alliance and the Climate Psychology Alliance North America have a directory of climate-aware therapists, as well as additional online resources.
In the United States: **climatepsychology.us/**
International: **climatepsychology-alliance.org/support/indsupport**

Helpline

SAMHSA Disaster Distress Helpline
1-800-985-5990

A 24/7, toll-free, year-round hotline providing crisis counseling and support to people experiencing emotional distress related to natural or human-caused disasters. Phone or text service available.

Carrie Lara, PsyD, is a licensed clinical psychologist who has worked with a range of clients, from children and families to adults with severe mental illness. She is an award-winning children's book author whose books include *Marvelous Maravilloso* and *The Heart of Mi Familia*. She lives in Sonoma County, CA with her family, where they have had first hand experience surviving the natural disaster of wildfires. Visit carrielara.com and @AuthorCarrieLara on Facebook and Instagram.

Colleen Larmour is a children's book illustrator and author. She graduated from the Cambridge School of Art masters course in children's book illustration. Her published titles include *Under the Silvery Moon*, *Little Friend*, *Making Friends: A Book About First Friendships*, and *Our Green City*. She lives in Northern Ireland. Visit her at colleenlarmour.com and @ColleenLarmour on Twitter and Instagram.

Magination Press is the children's book imprint of the American Psychological Association. APA works to advance psychology as a science and profession and as a means of promoting health and human welfare. Magination Press books reach young readers and their parents and caregivers to make navigating life's challenges a little easier. It's the combined power of psychology and literature that makes a Magination Press book special. Visit maginationpress.org and @MaginationPress on Facebook, Twitter, Instagram, and Pinterest.